D0041275

Praise for the writing of Christopher de Vinck

"More than any other author I know, Chris has the unique gift of revealing the beauty of the ordinary, the truth hidden in the small events of life, and the light shining through the brokenness of our daily existence. This book is a true gift of peace and an urgent call to discover that peace right where we live."

—HENRI J. M. NOUWEN

"Christopher is the rare combination of art and innocence. He's ever the sophisticated artist and he is even the person whose innocence belies our common conception of artists. Few spiritual writers write with as much literary talent and as much care for the literary quality of what they are doing."

—RONALD ROLHEISER

"Chris de Vinck is a blessing through his writing and his person. I'm grateful for his simple wonders, and the great wonders of our lifelong friendship."

—FRED ROGERS

"I would like as many people as possible to know his work."

—MADELEINE L'ENGLE

"Christopher de Vinck has the insight and the courage to speak for those small devotions, dangerously unfashionable in our time, by which a human community lives."

—WENDELL BERRY

"Christopher de Vinck's writings are widely and wisely attentive; they neglect neither the failures and anguish nor the compassion and hope of this world. They are elegant. They give insight and comfort. They cannot help but nurture the spirit."

—MARY OLIVER

"Chris de Vinck's real subject is magic, the magic to be found in ordinary life, in a conversation with a child, in the unexpected sighting of a school of dolphins. Such magic is there for all to see, but I don't know of another writer who sees it so wholly, with such consistency, and respect, and sweetness. He is like a miner who digs where others see no gold, and who each day finds riches."

—PEGGY NOONAN

MR. NICHOLAS
A Magical Christmas Tale

CHRISTOPHER DE VINCK

PARACLETE PRESS
Brewster, Massachusetts

2021 First Printing

Mr. Nicholas: A Magical Christmas Tale

Copyright © 2021 by Christopher de Vinck

ISBN 978-1-64060-735-4

Illustrations by Br. Philip MacNeil, CJ.

The Paraclete Press name and logo (dove on cross) are trademarks of Paraclete Press

Library of Congress Cataloging-in-Publication Data

Names: De Vinck, Christopher, 1951- author.
Title: Mr. Nicholas : a magical Christmas tale / Christopher de Vinck.
Description: Brewster, Massachusetts : Paraclete Press, [2021] | Summary:
  "A story that helps us see the unique goodness in each person. A boy
  with Down Syndrome, figures out that Mr. Nicholas, the local hardware
  store owner, involved with reindeer, toys, and children is more than
  just a clerk on Main Street"-- Provided by publisher.
Identifiers: LCCN 2021017319 | ISBN 9781640607354 (hardcover) | ISBN
  9781640607361 (epub) | ISBN 9781640607378 (pdf)
Subjects: LCSH: Christmas stories. | BISAC: FICTION / Christian /
  Contemporary | FICTION / Christian / Suspense
Classification: LCC PS3554.E11588 M7 2021 | DDC 813/.54--dc23
LC record available at https://lccn.loc.gov/2021017319

10 9 8 7 6 5 4 3 2 1

Published by Paraclete Press
Brewster, Massachusetts
www.paracletepress.com

Printed in the United States of America

To my daughter, Karen

"I stopped believing in Santa Claus when I was six.
My mother took me to see him in a department store
and he asked for my autograph."

—Shirley Temple

CONTENTS

FOREWORD

My husband truly believed that everyone was special. No matter your size, color, gender, orientation, no matter if you were a Harvard graduate or a child with Down syndrome, Fred treated each person with respect and dignity.

In this little book about Christmas, written by one of Fred's closest friends, you will see how *Mister Rogers' Neighborhood* spoke to the broken parts of who we are and how it guided us to see the unique goodness in us all.

Fred came home one afternoon from a visit with his favorite professor from seminary who was dying in a nursing facility. Fred loved the usual weekly visits with this remarkable friend, and this particular time Dr. Orr was thinking of the words of the well-known hymn by Martin Luther. In one line there is mention of "the Devil," and the words say, "One little word shall fell him." Fred was fascinated that Dr. William Orr said, "and that little word is FORGIVENESS!" That was a story that Fred took so greatly to heart and he told it many, many times.

This Christmas story is about forgiveness between a couple about to enact a divorce, and how their son with Down syndrome understood the power of seeing what is truly essential.

At the very foundation of Fred's television program, at the very foundation of his life as a husband, father, and friend, were the essential words of kindness, compassion, empathy, and, above all else, love.

May the charm of this little book add to the beauty of your neighborhood, and may you keep close to your hearts the Christmas gift that unfolds: the birth of a child in Bethlehem who, like Fred, reminded us that it is in the gift of love for one another that the true December mystery is revealed to us year after year.

—JOANNE ROGERS

MR. NICHOLAS

A Magical Christmas Tale

ONE
MARRIAGE

I never planned on getting married, and I never planned on heading for a divorce. Like the weather, divorce sneaks up on you like the misery of an advancing tornado.

I was a beat reporter for a local newspaper, driving along the rural hills of western Pennsylvania listening to an NPR program on the radio about Ringo Starr.

Ringo is my favorite Beatle because he always seemed to be the ignored one, at the edge of the fame, talent, and pandemonium that surrounded the group. That was me: ignored and filled with misplaced ambitions.

In an interview Ringo spoke about coming up from a working-class neighborhood in Liverpool to wearing a tuxedo at the movie premiere for *A Hard Day's Night*. I like how he said he was standing next to George Harrison, smoking a cigar. My idea of success was wearing a tuxedo, smoking a cigar, and standing next to George Harrison.

I was on my way to Green Meadow Farm to interview a beekeeper. The managing editor of the paper thought I would be a perfect reporter for the job, maybe because at the time I had a ponytail and was a vegetarian. Somehow beekeepers get a bad rap. All that talk of honey and the environment makes them sound like orphans of the sixties.

I had a poster of Henry David Thoreau hanging in my cubicle at work. There was Henry wearing a bowtie. His beard looked like my grandfather's beard and his face looked like the face of a principal ready to give a kid detention for smoking in the bathroom. Under the photograph were Henry's words: "The keeping of bees is like the direction of sunbeams." I had no idea what that meant. It sounded profound coming from a famous writer. I wanted to be a famous writer and say things that would impress people, and there I was driving a beat-up pickup truck on my way to interview a beekeeper.

So I was driving up and down along these Pennsylvania hills looking for Green Meadow Farm and preparing questions in my head to ask the beekeeper, a Mrs. Grace Davis. She had written a book about bees and was in her late eighties. I had a hard time juggling the map in my hand and keeping the car on the right side of the road. There are people today who don't even know what a map is.

I knew I had to go a few more miles and make a right at Old Stone Road and was afraid that I'd missed the turn. I was hoping to see the next road on the map when I noticed an old man standing near a crooked mailbox at the end of a driveway. I pulled up to the guy. He looked used up: white beard, red shirt, worn suspenders looped over his shoulder.

I turned my radio off and rolled down the passenger side window. "Excuse me. Can you tell me where Old Stone Road is? I think I'm lost."

The old man leaned into the window and said, "Lost? Who you seeing?"

"Mrs. Grace Davis. I'm a reporter. I'm going to interview her about her bees."

"Nice lady. Makes great cookies. Just keep going a bit farther. Next left, then follow the sunbeams."

"Sunbeams?" I asked, thinking he must have the same Thoreau poster.

"Just down the road." The old man stepped back from the car, and as I began to drive away I thought I heard him say, "Good luck, Jim." How did he know my name? But then I realized that it must have been my own voice hoping to find Old Stone Road.

I turned the radio on again and heard that just before the Beatles were coming to New York for their first concert a reporter asked Ringo, "So what do you think? How do you find America?" And Ringo answered with a straight face, "Turn left at Greenland and keep going." He didn't say anything about sunbeams.

Sure enough, the old man was right. Old Stone Road quickly appeared to my left. I turned onto the road and knew the bee farm was less than a mile away. I tossed the map onto the back seat and was about to shut off the radio when I saw to my right a car tilting precariously beside a ditch, and standing in front of the car was a young woman about my age.

NPR was playing, ironically, Ringo singing, *Don't pass me by, don't make me cry, don't make me blue.* I pulled up behind the lopsided car, turned off the engine to my car, opened the door, and asked the girl, "Are you all right? I saw your car."

"Oh. Hello. No, I'm fine. I just stopped to look at the view and those sheep."

I gazed across the field, and sure enough, there were sheep grazing on a deep green pasture in what looked like a painting right out of Norman Rockwell's studio.

"It looked like you were in trouble."

"No. I'm okay. I just had to stop and look at that hillside."

"Your car looked like it was falling into the ditch."

"I thought I came too close to the shoulder. I'm okay. I better be on my way."

The woman wore jeans, a flannel shirt, and an illuminating smile. Impulsively I said, "Well, as I see it, would you like to go to a play in New York with me, visit the Rodin Museum in Philadelphia, or go out to dinner."

She looked at me and said, "Yes. But how about we also go to Paris on a magic carpet."

"That too," I said.

That is how I met Anna. We exchanged phone numbers, and as I watched her drive away, I tucked her number into my pocket, grabbed my car keys, and drove up to a sign that read *Green Meadows Farm—Honey.*

Grace Davis gave me a tour of her hives and explained that honey is the only edible substance produced by any insect, that if stored properly, will never spoil, and will build up your immune system.

When I explained to Mrs. Davis that it was thanks to an old man down the road that I was able to find her farm, she said, "He's one of my best customers. I bake him cookies every Christmas Eve, but he loves my honey. I sometimes think that honey is all he eats. He probably has the strongest immune system that will make him immortal like my honey."

I wrote my story for the paper about Mrs. Davis and her bees, and the day it ran in the paper, Anna called and said she had bought two tickets to *Les Miserables* on Broadway. I wanted to see *Jersey Boys*.

We went to see *Les Miserables*, and when in the first act Fantine sang *I dreamed a dream in times gone by, when hope was high and life worth living,* Anna took my hand for the first time. On our second date, when we went to see the Rodin sculptures in Philadelphia, and as we stood in front of Rodin's most famous work, Anna turned and spontaneously kissed me. On our third date, after wine and sushi, she asked me in the restaurant to marry her. I said yes, and then we ordered dessert. We planned to go to Paris for our honeymoon, but I was too busy at the newspaper, so we just went to New York for two days. I suggested going to a Yankees game. Anna wanted to spend both days at the Metropolitan Museum of Art. To me, Tommy John's pitching style was far more beautiful than anything Rembrandt painted.

Anna was ambitious and wanted to paint. I was ambitious and wanted to write. After the *New York Times* hired me as an investigative reporter, we bought a small house in Pompton Plains, New Jersey, just a short bus ride from New York City. Anna began painting large flowers on wide canvases in the style of Georgia O'Keeffe.

We converted the basement into her studio, and one afternoon, during our third year of marriage, Anna asked me for an opinion on one of her paintings. I said, "It's okay. It looks a lot like a Georgia O'Keeffe flower." It was a large, purple iris. I don't know much about art, and that afternoon I began to discover that I didn't know much about Anna either. "And too much purple."

"Do you always have to criticize what I do?" she said, as she leaned over the studio sink to wash a brush. The water gushed from the faucet.

"You asked me if I like it. I said it's okay."

At a neighbor's Christmas Eve cocktail party Anna and I attended, Ida, our host, asked us each to share our greatest joy as she handed out glasses of wine. When it was my turn, I said my greatest joy was writing, and when it was Anna's turn, she looked at me as her eyes watered and said nothing.

"Let's go to the piano and sing some Christmas carols," Ida suggested.

On our way home in the car Anna said, "Let's try and have a baby."

I didn't know much about art, and I didn't know that Anna thought that having a baby might bring us closer together.

As we entered the house, I helped Anna with her coat, and I began to sing *I dreamed a dream in times gone by, when hope was high and life worth living.* Anna turned to me and asked, "Jim, do you really know who I am? I mean on the inside?"

I was afraid this was a trick question.

"We've been married for three years. You leave the house at six, you come home at six. You squeeze me in between football in the fall and between innings in baseball in the spring. I talk more to my painted flowers than I talk with you. Where are we going?"

I knew my work. I could dig into the depth of a political scandal. I knew the nuance of a quarterback sneak. I knew the value of statistics in baseball, but I did not know who I was. Marriage to me was just the next step in life, another merit badge to pin on my Boy Scout uniform. I fertilized my own lawn, never missed a day at work, made sure we had plenty of beer and potato chips in the house. I never had an epiphany, or an "ah-ha" moment that knocked me into a new way of seeing and living.

When I first saw Anna by the side of the road I was attracted to her; our dates were fun. We got married. She was pretty. She liked me. I liked her. I wanted to have fun. I didn't know at the time that she wanted me to pick irises with her. I wanted football. She wanted to talk.

When she asked me where we were going, I thought she meant where we were going on vacation for the summer.

"We are drifting apart, Jim."

"You read too many books," I said.

"Books talk to me more than you do."

"Anna, we talk."

"Yes, about the need to paint the house, or to buy a new car. I want to talk about us. You never ask me if I am lonely."

"Lonely? How can you be lonely? You have Ida and her friends. We're together."

"No one *sees* me, Jim."

"I see you all the time. I see you right now. You're not invisible."

"Jim, we need something that will connect us, and it's not football and my painting."

That is when we agreed to try for a baby. Anna was hoping I'd see things differently if we had a baby, and then she and I would grow closer.

But when JB was born, to me a baby was a baby and I just kept working, commuting back and forth between the city and our small town, watching football and eating potato chips.

TWO
JB

One thing about our town, it's small and intimate. The land, the buildings, the streets were designed and laid out back in the 1700s and 1800s. Everything was bought up and people had to make do. George Washington really did sleep here for a few nights during the American Revolution.

The hardware store is built right beside the eye doctor's place, and his place is right beside Annie Cooper's bookstore, and next to her place, the pizza parlor, then the hairdresser, and then the florist, and at the end of the street, Sally's Sweet

Shop. No room for anyone to expand in any direction.

On the other side of the hardware store is a barn, and behind the store an oak tree that hasn't budged in over two hundred years. So no matter how anyone sized things up, Nicholas' Hardware Store was one room deep and two rooms wide with a door to the basement. Unless the basement was the size of a football field, no one understood how old Mr. Nicholas could fit everything that he needed to satisfy his customers' requests. We all suspected something was odd about the store, but, like the board of education, once we knew it was there, we just didn't ask many questions and kept our opinions to ourselves.

Even I admit to not having paid as much attention, not only to Anna, but to the hardware store as I should have. As a reporter for the *New York Times,* it's my business to investigate mysterious events. I'd lived in this town for three years, commuting to my New York office, covering the crime beat, digging for facts, following up on leads. A reporter has to almost be born with curiosity and with the need to find things out. Perhaps I let down my guard when I was home, not caring much for my job or Anna, leaving my investigative instincts in the city. Too bad. The greatest scoop of the century waited for me right there under my nose, right in my own town, and I didn't know it. It took just one kid, a boy, to figure out all there was to know about Mr. Nicholas and his hardware store, and to figure out what was wrong with me and Anna.

Let me first tell you about JB. His real name is John Brian Kelly, but he wasn't very good at pronouncing words when he first learned to speak, so we just called him JB. He liked that. "JB hungry. JB pet dog? JB want ice cream." Everyone called him JB.

It was easy in the beginning when JB was born. I could hide my disgust for the boy from the public, but Anna saw it in my eyes when I held the baby in my arms for the first time. "What's wrong with his eyes?" I asked the doctor as he looked at Anna's chart a few hours after JB was born.

The doctor sat on the bed and looked up at me and said, "Mr. Kelly, you have a very special boy in your arms."

"Special? What do you mean, special?" I looked at my wife.

The doctor explained. "Your son has what is commonly referred to as Down syndrome. It involves a chromosomal abnormality."

As the doctor spoke, I looked at each part of JB's body.

"Persons with Down syndrome are often short in stature and have a small, round head with a high flattened forehead and fissured, dry lips and tongue."

I looked at JB's head and eyes. He stuck out his tongue for a second.

"A typical feature is a fold of skin, the epi-canthic fold, on either side of the bridge of the nose."

I looked at JB's nose.

"The palms show a single transverse crease, and the soles have a straight crease from the heel to the space between the first and second toes."

I looked at JB's feet.

"Many children like your son are subject to heart defects which can often be corrected surgically."

I looked up from the boy, I looked at Anna, and then I asked the doctor, "Well, can he play baseball?"

The doctor explained that most people with JB's condition go to school, and most adults even find jobs of various types. "JB will probably always have the intellect of an eight-year-old, but he will learn how to speak and play and be, in many ways, like most children you know."

"I don't know any children," I said. I was filled with confusion and disappointment as I handed the baby to my wife and walked out of the room.

The baby didn't bring Anna and me closer together. I could not accept how different this boy was. For ten years Anna was the one who went to all those meetings with other parents of special babies. She was the one who borrowed all the books from the library as she tried to learn all that she could about chromosomes, special education, patterning, diet, and exercise.

When JB was almost two, he hadn't yet spoken, and he had barely learned how to walk. During one particularly bitter night, after JB finally went to sleep at three o'clock in the morning, Anna asked me why I couldn't love my son. When I lamely said that I did love the boy, she asked me to define love. We were both in bed with the lights out. I remember the moon slid in between the sides of the drawn shade. "Well, I pay the bills, don't I?"

Anna turned to me. I could see her silhouette. "Do you *love* the boy?"

I wanted to tell her at the time that I could not accept his pudgy hands, his crooked lips, or his odd eyes. I wanted to tell her that the baby was not what I expected. A father wants Superboy for a son, a boy who can throw a football 50 or 60 yards, outrun a locomotive, or use his X-ray vision, but instead, all I said was, "Yeah, I love him."

Anna and I plodded along. The flowers that she painted grew smaller and smaller on the canvases, while my articles were being published on the front page of the paper and I was nominated for a Pulitzer. The prizes were announced on a Friday. I didn't win and just sulked that following Sunday, watching the Yankees on TV lose to Minnesota.

JB sat on the floor wearing his Yankees hat, and when the game was over, he had a sad look on his face and wanted to sit on my lap, but I pushed him away.

The next morning Anna said she had filed separation papers with a lawyer. So I blamed JB for that too. This small, confused set of chromosomes wiggled into the world, blinded my X-ray vision, grew up to a ten-year-old boy, and ruined my life.

A marriage counselor suggested that we go for a trial separation and meet with her once a week, so Anna kept the house and I rented an apartment in town, across from the hardware store above a lawyer's office, the same lawyer Anna had hired for the separation proceedings.

I was awarded visitation rights. I didn't even want visitation rights. I didn't care. The Yankees lost. I didn't win a Pulitzer. JB could have stayed in the house for the rest of his life as far as I was concerned, but no, every Friday evening Anna brought JB to my place.

One Friday, during the first month of our separation, Anna pulled up before my apartment and carried JB to the top of the stairs. I opened the door and took the boy from her arms. Anna reminded me to give JB his medication, to bathe him, and to let him watch *Mr. Rogers' Neighborhood*, and then she looked at me and said, "Our first meeting with the marriage counselor is next Tuesday at seven o'clock." She turned, walked back down the long, narrow stairs, stepped into her car, and drove home. A kid that doesn't look like Clark Kent comes into my life and my wife ends up in my house, and I have to go to a marriage counselor and pretend that I am filled with gushy feelings.

THREE
MARRIAGE COUNSELOR

"So, Mr. Kelly, my name is Brenda Matthews."

"You can call me Jim."

"So, Jim, what would you like to start off by saying? When Anna first contacted me, all she said was that her marriage was in trouble."

I looked at Anna. She sat beside me with her hands folded on her lap. I glanced up at a degree hanging on the wall: COLUMBIA UNIVERSITY: BRENDA MATTHEWS, DOCTOR OF PSYCHOLOGY. I sat on the couch with my arms folded. "I like baseball."

Anna shook her head. "That's what you want to start with? Baseball?" Anna turned and looked at Dr. Matthews. "See what I mean?"

"What's that supposed to mean?" I asked, unfolding my arms as I pleaded with my hands.

"It means you have no imagination, no heart." Anna raised her voice. "You skim on the surface of life and don't dream."

"I have plenty of dreams." I raised my voice. "I dream the Yankees will win the World Series and that I have a wife who supports me in my hopes of winning a Pulitzer Prize."

"Anna," Dr. Matthews interjected, "Anna. Maybe we can express our wishes calmly."

"Jim. I want to be your World Series win. JB wants to be your Pulitzer Prize."

I looked at my wife. I looked at the marriage counselor. "What's wrong with my wanting to be a bit selfish? I enjoy sports. I want to climb the career ladder. A happy wife is a happy life, they say. Well, a happy husband is also a happy life as well."

"Jim," Dr. Matthews asked, "did you have a make-believe world when you were a child?"

"Here we go. I was waiting for this. So typical. Dig up my past and see if you find any skeletons. A make-believe world? Who needs all that fake stuff? I thought we were here to talk about how to save our marriage, not to talk about fantasy land."

After the session, as Anna and I walked down the steps of the doctor's office, she said, "When I was a little girl I built my own doll house with a shoebox."

"Was it an Adidas or Puma box?" I asked without thinking.

Anna stopped, and sighed. "I'll see you on Friday, Jim."

As the months slowly progressed, Anna stopped carrying JB up those steps to my apartment. She'd hold his hand and he would lead her up. As a ten-year-old JB finally learned how to make it up the stairs by himself. Anna wouldn't even step out of the car. I only saw her at the counselor's office once a week.

One evening after JB's bath, I tied a red towel around his shoulder and called him Superboy. When JB smiled, I looked into his eyes for the first time and I smiled too.".

FOUR

MR. NICHOLAS

Everything bothered me at the time: people who swerved in and out of lanes on the highway, robocalls, incompetence at work. Contemporary music to me was nothing but a lot of screaming and the boom, boom, boom beat of a drum. I'd look at a modern painting of a horse, and to me it looked like a broken cube with teeth and one eye. I already had a broken kid in my life. I didn't need to be bothered by anything else that was odd, but just as my luck would have it, there was this odd man in our town that no one could help but notice.

Mr. Nicholas was odd. There is no doubt whatsoever about that. He had two occupations: scavenger and proprietor of the hardware store at the corner of the Newark-Pompton Turnpike and Jackson Avenue.

Every Friday morning Mr. Nicholas would drive up and down the streets of our little town in his red 1929 Ford Model A pick-up truck. The truck made a clanking, clucking noise that sounded like a hundred children imitating a hundred chickens: cluck, chug, cluck, chug. Cluck, bang, cluck, cluck, cluck. Just like that. And just like that, every Friday morning, Mr. Nicholas would wake everyone up at four o'clock in the morning as he made his rounds up and down the street in his red antique truck, stopping at each driveway and inspecting all of the non-recyclable material. Cluck, chug, cluck, chug. Cluck, bang, cluck, cluck, cluck. And when Mr. Nicholas would stop and shift his truck into neutral, it seemed to sound like a cat purring with a hiccup. Purr. Purr. Hiccup. Hiccup, and the truck would jitter slightly back and forth.

Each time Mr. Nicholas stopped at the end of a driveway and stepped out of the truck, he would walk to the front and gently pat the large round headlights one at a time as if he were soothing a happy but tired horse. It was reported that many people actually believed that each time Mr. Nicholas touched the headlight, the truck stopped jittering and the lights blinked in gratitude. I just thought he was odd.

The town posted strict rules about the collection of solid waste: all usual garbage will be picked up on Mondays. All recyclable materials will be picked up on Wednesdays. All other items will be collected on Fridays.

It was obvious which items Mr. Nicolas was especially interested in collecting: bicycles, broken dolls, model train engines with missing wheels, old swing sets, discarded model ships, plastic airplanes, marbles, the ribs of large kites, cracked piggy banks, miniature safes with broken combination locks . . . broken children's toys. Who wanted broken children's toys? Odd.

When his truck was filled, he'd drive to his hardware store, and as he drove he'd wave to the early milkman, and to the policeman on the corner. Children in their pajamas would run to their windows and wave. As Mr. Nicholas drove by their homes he'd press his chubby hand onto the horn button of his red truck, and the truck would groan and giggle a loud "Ah-Ooh-GA." Mr. Nicholas would wave to the children as if he were running for mayor, and the children would wave back as if they were sure to give him their votes.

If JB happened to be over on a Friday morning, he'd come bouncing onto my bed to announce, "Mr. Nicholas is coming! Mr. Nicholas is coming! I hear him coming!" I'd roll over and growl like a dog. "Go to the front window, JB. Let me sleep some more."

Those mornings, JB would scramble off the bed, salute, and run down the hall to the window at the front of the apartment to wait for Mr. Nicholas and the red truck.

JB liked the truck and the way Mr. Nicholas waved. The town didn't like the truck's pollution or the noise it made so early in the morning, and they did not like that Mr. Nicholas was, well, odd.

FIVE
SUSPICION

I should have acted on my suspicions, but I didn't. The mayor said all along he knew that there was something odd about Mr. Nicholas, but he didn't want to alarm the citizens. The priests and ministers each felt, separately, there was something unusual about the hardware store, but they continued preaching in their churches and, at night, scratching their heads, wondering.

The postal workers were not allowed to speak about their concerns, for, as federal employees, they were hired to accept parcels and letters and deliver them from one point to the next. It was not their right to shake the packages or to place envelopes up to a lamp and try to read what was said, but the clerks in the post office did take extra notice when certain packages and letters were accepted at the window.

The police were never notified, but they too suspected more was going on in the hardware store than just the selling of paint and garden rakes. Often, as they drove down Main Street, they looked into the window hoping to see something strange, but all they saw, night after night, was Mr. Nicholas sitting at his desk, working on his accounts.

I learned that everyone in town felt a certain uneasiness about the blue building with rust-colored shutters. In the winter, snow shovels, bags of rock salt, and sacks of bird feed leaned against the outside wall, just to the left of the front door, indicators that Mr. Nicholas was open for business. In the summer, at 8:00 a.m sharp, he carried out watering cans and rakes, and he rolled out wheelbarrows and lawn spreaders.

Perhaps every house in town was held together in one way or another with screws, wires, door hinges, washers, clamps, bricks, two-by-fours, nails, tar, rope, all bought from Mr. Nicholas. He was a short, round man with a trimmed beard. He wore red suspenders, took his vacation in December, wasn't married, and gave all children who came into the hardware store a piece of chocolate wrapped in gold foil. The chocolate pieces were always a different shape: an airplane, a tricycle, a balloon, a robot, a cat, a horse, a kite.

On most Saturday mornings there'd be a line of customers from the front counter all the way down the aisle and sometimes out the door. Mr. Nicholas would stand at the front of the line with a white pad of paper and a pencil and write down what it was that we needed: a pound of nails or a gallon of paint; a chisel, brackets, bug repellent, tacks, hammers, shingles, locks, doorbells, a weather vane, a mailbox, cement, lime, bird feeders, fertilizer, telephone wire, light switches, fuses, light bulbs, plungers, thermo-stats, key chains, saw blades, flower pots, sandpaper, varnish, grout, a wheel for a barrow, a light reflector for a bicycle, paint brushes, bolts, mousetraps.

No matter what we asked for, Mr. Nicholas would write it on his white pad, look up and think for a few seconds, then step out from behind his counter, squeeze between everyone waiting, reach up, and find what it was that we needed. If the item, a power drill for example, was not on the first floor, Mr. Nicholas would politely excuse himself, open a green door and disappear down a narrow stairwell into the basement. Moments later, he'd reappear with the new drill.

One December morning, as JB, twelve other townspeople, and I were all standing in line, Charlie Danker said, "Mr. Nicholas, I need a Weil-McLain furnace."

We peered over Charlie's shoulder and watched Mr. Nicholas write on the pad in his formal script: *one Weil-McLain furnace*, and then he looked up from the paper, thought a bit, and disappeared into the basement. JB pulled my coat sleeve and asked in a loud voice, "Can I have chocolate?"

"It's not polite to ask, JB. We'll just have to wait and see."

"You need a furnace?" Dr. Brown asked Charlie.

"I've been coming in here for twenty-five years," Charlie said, "and no matter what I've ever asked for, Mr. Nicholas came up with it."

"Same here," Tom said, our local IRS agent. "I don't know how he does it."

We all agreed. Mr. Nicholas was always able to fill each order we gave him.

"I want a piece of chocolate," JB said.

"I don't need a furnace. I don't want a furnace," Charlie said. "I just thought I'd order one of the biggest items that popped into my head. Just once I'd like to see what Mr. Nicholas would do when he couldn't come up with what I asked for."

JB looked up at me with his moon-twisted face and licked his lips.

"I know, JB. Chocolate."

After a few moments, we heard the sound of footsteps coming up the basement stairs, and when the door opened, fifteen people stared at the man with the red suspenders. We followed him with our eyes as he returned to the front of his counter, picked up his pencil and licked the point. He looked up at Charlie. We all leaned forward a bit as we heard Mr. Nicholas say, "That'll be six hundred seventy-five dollars." Then he nodded toward the window just beyond his desk and wrote the price onto the pad. There on the sidewalk sat a new Weil-McLain furnace. It was blue.

Charlie gazed out that window as if he had seen an elephant dancing on its nose, then he looked at all of us, scratched his head, turned to Mr. Nicholas and said, "Put it on my bill." Then he huffed and puffed his way between us, walked out the store, and slammed the door behind him. After I bought a can of paint, Mr. Nicholas turned to JB and said, "See you soon, JB," and winked as he handed JB a piece of chocolate wrapped in gold foil. It was a deer.

From that day forward, no one in town ever questioned Mr. Nicholas's inventory capabilities. But we were all puzzled.

When I thought about the way the town judged Mr. Nicholas on appearances, I felt a sudden sense of regret when I realized I did the same thing when JB was born.

SIX

DARTH VADER

A week had gone by, and I had to endure the second session with Anna at the marriage counselor's office, even though I had received in the mail the legal separation papers.

"Jim, a week has gone by. Have you given any thought to our first session?"

"Yeah. I can't be what Anna wants me to be."

"And what's that?" Dr. Matthews asked.

I looked at Anna. "There is this nutty guy in our town who collects broken toys. JB watches that kids' show *Mr. Rogers' Neighborhood*. Anna, you want me to be more whimsical, creative—I don't remember what you said."

"You don't dream, Jim," Anna said. "You don't see me. I feel like I am invisible. I don't feel as if you love me anymore."

That stopped me. "I have never been much of a person to say I love you to anyone. I thought that if you were with someone and liked being together, you didn't have to say I love you every minute."

"It's not that. I want to feel safe with you, vulnerable. How can I be with a man who pays more attention to his work and baseball than to me and his son?"

"Jim," Dr. Matthews asked, "do you want to save your marriage?"

When I sat there and didn't respond, Anna cried, stood up, and walked out of the office.

The next night I looked out my window at exactly 6:30, the same time every Friday evening. Anna, as usual, honked the horn of her van. The front passenger door opened, and JB tumbled out and landed on his feet. He reached in for his duffel bag and his Star Wars lunch box. I opened my door and looked down those stairs as JB clambered up like a fireman. A pudgy, goofy fireman with a Star Wars lunch box. As JB reached the top of the stairs, he looked up at me, saluted, and said, "Hi, Darth Vader." Then he ran into the living room and turned on the television set.

It's such a good feeling to know you're alive. It's such a happy feeling: you're growing inside. I rolled my eyes. JB knew all the words to Mr. Rogers' songs. When Mr. Rogers waved the fish food over the tank of water, JB waved his own hand over an imaginary fish tank and pretended he was sprinkling food to his pretend goldfish.

That night a violent jolt to my bed woke me. I opened my eyes, and there was JB sitting beside me. "Darth Vader! We gotta feed the fish," he whispered.

"JB, it's the middle of the night."

He grinned as he placed my face between his fat hands and said, "We gotta feed the fish. We forgot ta feed them." Then he took my hand and tried pulling me out of bed.

"All right." I pushed back my covers and allowed JB to lead me into the living room. He scrambled onto the couch like a monkey, and then he patted the cushion beside him. I sat down next to JB, in the semi-darkness. He pinched out a bit of imaginary fish food from an imaginary box and sprinkled the imaginary food into the imaginary tank of imaginary fish. He waved his hand out before him in a slow, back-and-forth motion.

"They're goldfish," JB informed me. "Just like Mr. Rogers' fish." He leaned over and handed me the box of imaginary fish food. "Your turn."

I looked at JB's hand.

"You gotta get a bit between your fingers."

I reached into the imaginary box and pinched just enough imaginary fish food and sprinkled it on the calm surface of the imaginary water. JB looked up and said, "They were hungry."

I carried JB back to bed, and when I leaned over to adjust his pillow, he whispered, "Good night, Darth Vader."

"Good night, JB," I said. It was at that moment that I saw a light in JB's face, beyond a smile, a sweetness that I didn't realize was there all along.

That night, after JB went to bed I called Anna on the phone and apologized for my silence at the counselor's office. "I do want to try and save the marriage, Anna."

"I don't think you are capable of it, Jim. I just don't see how you could possibly understand what it is that divides us."

"I helped JB feed imaginary fish."

"What?"

"JB, he saw Mr. Rogers feeding the goldfish, so JB and I, JB wanted me to help him feed the fish."

This time Anna was silent.

"Anna, are you still there?"

"I just feel like I'm on an emotional roller-coaster, Jim. I'll see you next week." And she hung up the phone.

SEVEN

BAMBI

JB seemed to know things, or at least he pretended to know. Maybe he did have X-ray vision. He could be sitting in the living room coloring and he'd say, "Someone's at the door." I don't have a doorbell, but sure enough I'd go to the front door and there would be the delivery boy with the pizza, or Anna, or my neighbor with my mail. He'd wake me up in the middle of the night to feed his imaginary fish, or say someone in town sustained an injury, and I'd find out the next day that one of his teachers had burned herself on a toaster oven, or Anna had fallen and injured her knee.

"Darth Vader," JB said on his birthday. "There's a dead bee in my lunch box." When I went to JB's shelf in the kitchen, I pulled down his Star Wars lunch box, flipped open the lid and found a wasp stuck in the sticky mass of an uneaten jelly sandwich. When I stepped up to JB and showed him the dead wasp, he reached over with his hand, placed the insect on his paper napkin, and rolled it carefully into a small parcel.

"Let's bury the bee," JB said. He tumbled from the kitchen chair and opened the drawer where I kept the silverware.

"What are you looking for, JB?"

"A shovel," he said triumphantly, as he produced a large soupspoon.

As we stooped over the freshly opened earth behind my apartment, JB said, "Say a prayer."

"I don't know any prayers, JB."

He looked up at me with his slanted eyes and with his twisted smile, and then he patted the ground where he had just buried the wasp and said, "I like you just the way you are. You are special. Goodbye, bee. Amen." JB continued, "Mr. Rogers tells me that all the time just before he says goodbye."

JB and I both said goodbye to the wasp.

The second time JB met Mr. Nicholas was in the middle of the night, after JB had another one of his premonitions.

"Darth Vader," JB whispered, as I slept in my bed. "Darth Vader." I slowly opened my eyes to find JB fully dressed. He was also wearing my sombrero, a gift from a Mexican friend who liked one of my essays about our immigrant policy in Texas. JB also had a flashlight in his right hand.

"We have to find Bambi."

JB had an imagination. And he was impressionable. Combine those two forces and you had a Down syndrome boy who, if he watched Mary Poppins flying with an umbrella, would spend the next week carrying an umbrella with him and telling everyone that he was flying. He was the Ronald McDonald clown for two weeks, asking everyone he met if they wanted a hamburger. JB heard the Beatle lyric "I am the walrus" at his uncle's house one night, and when we explained to JB that a walrus is a giant seal, and after he saw a walrus on the Nature Channel, well, he wouldn't walk properly for days. He dragged himself around with his arms, letting his legs slosh along the floor. We had to ask JB what he was, and each time he would say with a grin, "I am the walrus, coo, coo, ca, choo."

The day I rented the Disney film *Bambi* for JB, he woke up in the middle of the night convinced that Bambi was in distress. "The fire's going to get him," he said under the fringe of the sombrero.

"JB, that was in the movie. Remember seeing the movie with Thumper?"

"Thumper's home. Bambi's lost. We got to go help him." Then JB flicked on the flashlight and aimed it right into my left eye.

"All right. We'll go find Bambi."

Once JB was awake, no matter what time of day or night, it was difficult for him to fall back to sleep. Sometimes I found him watching television at three in the morning. I dressed.

"We'll go to Quick Check for some ice cream." JB liked ice cream, and I thought the twenty-minute ride there and back in the car would lull him to sleep.

"Can I have a chocolate cone?" JB asked.

"With sprinkles?" I added.

JB agreed. "Bring a hat," he said, as he walked to the front door and stood there waiting for me.

I slipped into my jeans and a sweatshirt, tied my boots and grabbed a Yankees cap, and we were off at 2:00 a.m. in search of ice cream, sleep . . . and Bambi.

"Want to take off your hat?" I asked JB as we drove down the street.

"I don't want my hair to catch fire," he said.

There was no moon, and the clouds hid the stars. The closest 24-hour food mart was down the highway a few miles. As I drove, the small balls hanging on the fringe of JB's sombrero jiggled up and down a bit.

"Don't drive in the fire," he warned.

We drove for a few miles alone in the darkness until, suddenly, we saw a pickup truck off to the side of the highway with its emergency lights flashing. I cautiously approached, wondering if someone needed help, or if someone might jump out at us. A heavyset man stood before the headlights of the parked truck. He was leaning over, looking at something in the ditch. I pulled up in front of the truck and stopped.

"JB. You stay in the car." He gave me a salute as he handed me his flashlight. "Right."

I stepped out from my car and walked over to the man who, by this time, was already making his way down the ditch. "Give me a hand," he said, as he looked up toward me. I aimed JB's flashlight into the man's face. "Mr. Nicholas?"

"Oh, it's you, Mr. Kelly," he said as he waved. I snapped off the light and slid down the embankment to his side.

"What is it?" I asked, as I noticed a sudden movement in the tall grass.

"I couldn't sleep," Mr. Nicholas said. "I was on my way to the food store when I saw a deer. It jumped right out from the other side of the highway. A car hit it. It staggered over to my side of the road and disappeared down the hill just as I stopped."

Mr. Nicholas turned from me and walked through the grass. I heard heavy breathing and snorting as Mr. Nicholas approached a dark mass lying in the ditch. "It's still alive," he said, as he called me over with the flashlight. "Shine it down by his legs." I aimed the light at the animal's rear legs and saw blood. Mr. Nicholas stooped down, reached out with his right hand, and whistled in a low pitch. The deer suddenly lay motionless as Mr. Nicholas ran his hand along its right leg.

"I don't think it's broken. We have to get him into the truck."

It was a small deer with a full set of antlers. As Mr. Nicholas leaned over, prepared to lift the back of the animal, he said, "You lift from the neck and head. Don't worry about the antlers. He won't hurt you," and then he whistled again in a low, soft manner.

I jammed the flashlight in my back pocket, and then I bent over and scooped my hands under the deer's neck.

"On the count of three," Mr. Nicholas directed. "One. Two. Three." And the two of us lifted the deer and began carrying it up the embankment. As I was struggling for a sure footing, I looked up and there was JB, standing in the headlight of the pickup truck, staring down at us from underneath his sombrero.

"You saved Bambi!" JB shouted, as he picked the hat from his head and waved it back and forth.

"That's my son," I said, as Mr. Nicholas and I cautiously made our way up the loose dirt and gravel. "He watches too many movies. He thinks we saved Bambi."

We slipped a bit, regained our balance, and shuffled the weight of the deer in our arms. My back felt the strain of the burden. When we reached the top of the rise, JB returned the sombrero to his head, looked at Mr. Nicholas and said, "Hello, Santa Claus."

"Hello, JB," Mr. Nicholas replied.

As Mr. Nicholas and I made our way to the back of the truck, I said, "He calls *me* Darth

Vader. JB makes up names for everyone. He's got Down syndrome."

"No, Jim. He's got you."

I looked at JB in his sombrero, and he giggled, a true, happy-boy giggle.

"Jim, can you reach over and open the tail-gate?" Mr. Nicholas asked.

"No, I don't think so," I said, as I looked at my JB and I giggled too.

"Do you think your son could do it?"

"JB," I asked, "do you think you could crawl into the truck and help open the back?"

Without hesitation, JB scrambled up over the seat and the side panel and, as Mr. Nicholas explained, he was able to pull a lever, and the tailgate slowly dropped open.

After we slid the injured deer onto the back of the truck, Mr. Nicholas reached up and shook JB's hand. "Good work."

JB saluted.

"Why don't you stop by my store tomorrow and check on the deer's progress?"

JB looked down at me. "Can I?"

"Sure. Tomorrow afternoon we'll come by."

"Thanks for your help," Mr. Nicholas said, as he shook my hand. He walked over and thanked JB again with a wink. JB winked back. Then Mr. Nicholas hopped into his truck and drove off. The deer lifted its head for a second, looking in my direction. JB waved.

When I carried JB up the stairs to my apartment that night I thought about the first time I held JB when he was born. Mr. Nicholas was right. JB didn't have Down syndrome, he had me.

I tucked him in bed without bothering to wash the chocolate ice cream from his chin. I didn't want to wake him.

EIGHT
ANNA

Early Monday morning, Anna called. "Do you think it is a good idea keeping JB up all hours of the night?"

"Anna, he couldn't sleep."

"Roaming around on the highway at two in the morning? Do you call that responsible behavior? JB told me everything."

"It wasn't my idea to have joint custody. You thought it was a good idea that he had a father. Well, I never planned JB. I never planned what happened to us. I thought things would be different, so I can't fix things now."

"Jim, what ten-year-old boy has a chocolate ice-cream cone in the middle of the night?"

"Did he also tell you that we went hunting for bear with a sling shot?"

"Are you telling me he made up what he said?" Anna's voice was steady.

"JB does tend to exaggerate."

"About the deer and the man with a white beard? JB said that you and a man with a white beard carried a deer into a truck. Did he make that up too?"

"No, Anna. We were on our way to the milk store when we found Mr. Nicholas. You know him. He runs the hardware store."

"Yes, of course, the most *sane* man in town."

"What's that supposed to mean?"

"Leave it to you to introduce my son to the oddest person around."

"Anna!"

"You know perfectly well, Jim, that Mr. Nicholas has a reputation. Rumors have been circulating through town ever since he came here. I don't like it. He keeps to himself, humiliates people, and apparently stays up all hours of the night driving around in his truck picking up dead deer."

"The deer wasn't dead. And when did Mr. Nicholas ever humiliate anyone?"

"I heard how Charlie asked for a furnace, and Mr. Nicholas sold him one."

"Charlie asked for a furnace and Mr. Nicholas accommodated a customer. Isn't that how business is done?"

"There is just a lot of talk about the man. Even the police are keeping an eye on him."

"Anna, the man is a bit different. I am trying to change, to do something about our marriage. I am trying to have that imagination you keep talking about. I am trying to see things you. . . . I don't know. Since when do *you* worry about people who are different?"

"Maybe since I discovered how different you are from the man I thought I married."

"What's that supposed to mean?"

"How hypocritical, Jim. You accuse me of condemning a man because he's a bit odd, and you can't even accept your own son."

"What gave you the idea that Mr. Nicholas is odd?"

"Open your eyes, Jim. Don't you see how he treats children? Everyone sees it. He has this spell over them or something. You can't say you don't see it."

"The man gives the children a treat whenever they come into the store. He jokes with them. But that doesn't make him odd."

"He just seems more interested in children than in adults. Yes. I call that odd and suspicious behavior. I don't want my son hanging around him."

"Well, I promised JB we'd go visit the deer we saved. Mr. Nicholas is keeping it in a pen behind his store."

"I'll not have it," Anna said.

"Look. I agreed to take JB on weekends. He's my responsibility too. We're just going to see a mangy deer. I don't see what harm there is in it."

"I just don't like it. The man is odd."

"Just bring the boy Friday night like you usually do. I have to go to work."

"I suggest that you not drag him out after midnight."

"Goodbye, Anna."

"Goodbye."

As I sat in my seat with other commuters on the bus heading for New York City, I looked out the window. As we passed the hardware store, I saw Mr. Nicholas lean over and pick up Charlie's eight-year-old daughter, place her on his shoulders, and follow Charlie into the store.

NINE

THE PHONE CALL

The first thing JB said when he climbed the stairs with his Star Wars lunch box Friday night was, "Can we go see the deer?"

JB had a deep voice, and when he spoke, his tongue rolled with the sounds of his letters in a way that made him sound just a bit off in his speech pattern. He had a speech teacher in school, and she helped him. At first I didn't think JB sounded like a normal child. Although he was ten, he acted four. The doctors said that there was a good chance that JB would be four all his life. He liked to chase cats, eat ice cream, slide on the floor in his socks, press his nose against the windowpane, and sleep with his panda bear (my birthday present to him). JB liked to be read to, he enjoyed sticking his finger into a bowl of Jell-O, he never missed watching *Mr. Rogers' Neighborhood*, and he was a nag. With each new day, JB sounded more and more normal to me.

"When are we going to see the deer?"

"Tomorrow, JB. Mr. Nicholas said it was best to come on Saturday night after he closes the store for the weekend."

"Can we just go now?"

"JB, Mr. Nicholas doesn't want us to come now."

"Can we go after *Mr. Rogers?*"

I sat on the floor beside JB and looked him in the eyes. "JB, we're going to have dinner, then I'll read to you a bit, then it will be time for bed. We'll go see the deer tomorrow."

We ate dinner: hamburgers, fries, and Jell-O. After JB stuck his finger into his bowl of Jell-O, and after he carried his plate to the sink, he looked up at me and said, "All done."

"Yes, very good."

"Now can we go see the deer?"

That night I read aloud *Ferdinand the Bull* and when I adjusted his pillow and blanket before he went to sleep, JB asked, "Did they bury the bumble bee Ferdinand sat on, like we did?"

"I don't know, JB." And then I remembered the counselor asking about a make-believe world. "Let's pretend that they did."

"I wouldn't want to sit on a bee," he said, as he closed his eyes.

"Good night, JB," I said.

"Good night, Darth Vader."

I shut off the light and closed his door.

Four hours later the phone rang, waking me up from my sleep. I looked at the clock as I grabbed the receiver: 2:47.

"Mr. Kelly?"

"Yes, this is Jim Kelly."

"Mr. Kelly, this is Sergeant Marino with the police department."

"Yes?"

"Everything is all right," the policeman said.

"Yes?"

"Would you come to the hospital? Your son has been in an accident. It took a bit of doing to figure out who he belonged to. We also called your wife. She's already on her way."

"But my son is sleeping in the next room," I said, as if I were suddenly sinking in an invisible fish tank, struggling to breathe.

"Mr. Kelly, please just come right away."

"Yes, OK, thank you." I returned the receiver to the phone's cradle.

"JB? JB!" I yelled as I slid across the floor in my socks. JB's bedroom door was open, his panda bear was on the floor, and his bed was empty.

TEN
FANTASY

"Dr. Green. Dr. Green. Please call maternity. Dr. Green. Dr. Green. Maternity."

The hospital loudspeaker brought some reality to where I was as I stepped up to the desk at the emergency room.

"May I help you?" a woman in a white uniform politely asked.

"My name is Mr. Kelly, Jim Kelly. I'm here for my son?"

"Let me check," the woman said, as she shuffled through a pile of papers on her desk. "Oh, yes, JB. He's in room 4-D. Your wife is already there."

I thanked the woman and ran down the hall. 4-A. 4-B. 4-C. 4-D. I stepped into the room and found Anna sitting on a chair next to the bed, and in the bed was JB. He was asleep with a bandage around his right arm.

"What happened?" I asked as I leaned over JB.

"That's a good question, Jim," Anna hissed. "I'd like to know exactly what happened. Maybe you can start explaining what a ten-year-old boy was doing wandering the streets by himself in the middle of the night."

"Anna. I read to him last night. We had dinner. He went to bed. I went to bed. That's all I know. He's never snuck out of the house before. You know that. I couldn't have known this would happen."

"You never seem to know when much happens around you."

"Now that's not fair. I do the best I can."

"Well, obviously 'the best you can' gets your son a bruised arm."

"How did it happen?"

"He said that he fell off a deer."

"What?"

"JB made up another one of his stories and said that he fell off a deer. He said that he was behind the hardware store on the back of that filthy creature you pulled off the highway last week. Anyway, that's JB's story. He said he was riding the deer, then he slipped off and hurt his arm."

"And you don't believe that?"

"Jim, he also said that he and the deer were flying around the oak tree."

"Well, you know about JB's imagination."

"Yes, I do, and that's what worries me. He comes up with fantastic stories when he doesn't want to tell the truth, or he is too afraid to tell the truth. All I know for sure is Mr. Nicholas brought my son to the hospital with a bleeding arm and here I am. Before they gave JB a sedative, he said when the deer stopped flying, it stumbled a bit on the landing and threw him to the ground. JB said how soft and warm the deer felt. I warned you about that crazy man, Jim, and now look what's happened."

"The boy just wanted to see the deer. I promised him we would see it tomorrow after Mr. Nicholas closed up the store, then JB went to bed. He had it in his mind to see the deer tonight. You know how stubborn JB is."

"I know that I don't know the whole story here, and I mean to find out. You know perfectly well that JB doesn't think like you and I do. He talks about soft things and feeling warm, and riding a deer and flying around a tree. Who knows what he's suppressing? Who knows what really happened? I just know Mr. Nicholas doesn't belong in this town, driving his truck at all hours of the night, inviting children to his store after hours, selling Charlie an oil furnace he doesn't need or want. JB's arm is badly bruised. It could have been his neck. I called the police."

"Yes, I know. Sergeant Marino called me."

"And they promised me they would make an investigation."

"Anna. The man is old. He's kind to children. He doesn't have any family. He's harmless."

"Yes. Look at this boy in bed and tell me Mr. Nicholas is harmless."

"JB has an imagination, a fantasy world. Maybe I can learn things from him. He makes me smile."

"What's that?" Anna asked.

"JB, he makes me smile."

Anna softened her eyes.

"He's a lot like you, Anna, filled with a rich imagination, and he's a lot like me, stubborn, but he comes around."

"Well, just be careful, Jim. JB will always be a fragile child. See you next week with Dr. Matthews?"

"I'll be there," I said, as I gently touched Anna's hand.

ELEVEN

THE FIRST INVESTIGATION

It was difficult to defend JB's tale about falling off the deer, but the next morning, JB stuck to his story.

"I wasn't afraid," he told me, as I pushed his wheelchair out through the open hospital doors. "It was just like Ferdinand."

"What was just like Ferdinand, JB?" I asked, as I helped him into the car.

"The deer. I wasn't afraid. You read how Ferdinand the bull wasn't mean. I knew that deer would be just like Ferdinand, so I climbed on its back. I just hoped the deer wouldn't sit on a bumble bee."

"Is that what happened, JB, when you fell?" I asked, as I slid into the driver's seat and started the car. "Did the deer sit on a bee?"

"Nope. After we flew around the tree we landed and I fell off. I think his leg still hurts."

We drove by the hardware store. The rock salt and snow shovels were in a neat row to the left of the front door. Mr. Nicholas was open for business as usual.

I drove JB to his mother's house. There was a police car in the driveway.

"Jim, this is Ben Marino," Anna said, as she led JB to the living room.

"We spoke on the phone last night," the policeman said.

"Yeah. Hello." We shook hands.

"I just want to ask you a few questions, then I'll be on my way, Mr. Kelly."

"Shoot. No, I mean, go ahead."

"About what time would you say that you went to sleep last night?"

"Oh, after sending JB to bed, I watched the ten o'clock news. I went to bed after that, a little after eleven o'clock."

"And you didn't know your son left the house until I called?"

"Right. He's never done this before."

"And how long has JB known Mr. Nicholas?"

I looked into the living room and saw JB and Anna sitting together on the couch watching cartoons.

"Well, I don't think he really knows the man. He met him for the first time a few weeks ago."

"What were the circumstances?" Sergeant Marino asked.

"The first time was at Mr. Nicholas's store. He gave JB some chocolate."

"And there was another time he was with the boy?"

"JB couldn't sleep last Friday night so I was taking him out for an ice-cream cone."

"What time was that?"

"Oh, about three o'clock."

"In the afternoon?" the policeman asked.

"Well, no. You see, once JB is awake, it's a little hard for him to go back to sleep, so I thought a ride in the car would make him drowsy, and I thought he'd like the idea of a bit of ice cream, you know, an incentive to get him into the car."

"At three o'clock in the morning, he had an ice-cream cone?" The policeman looked into the living room. "Then what happened?"

"Well we were driving, and I saw Mr. Nicholas on the side of the road. I didn't know it was Mr. Nicholas, but when I stopped to help, I recognized him. He saw a car hit a deer and I helped him carry the deer to his truck."

"Your son says that he has known Mr. Nicholas for as long as he can remember."

"JB doesn't remember what happened two days ago. He's got Down syndrome."

"Have you noticed anything strange about Mr. Nicholas, Mr. Kelly?"

"Well, no. He has a lot of stuff in his store. Everyone knows that. He keeps to himself a lot."

"Has he ever hurt JB?"

"He just met JB. He asked JB to help with the tailgate of the truck as we were carrying the deer. JB was wearing a sombrero."

"A sombrero?" Officer Marino asked as he looked up from his notepad.

"Yeah. It has this fringe with these little balls hanging down. JB was afraid of the fire."

"Fire?"

"We were watching *Bambi* that night, and JB was afraid after the part about the forest fire that killed Bambi's mother, so he wore the sombrero to protect his head from the fire. I wore my Yankees baseball cap."

Sergeant Marino stopped writing in his pad, looked at me and said, "You work for a newspaper?"

"Yes, the *New York Times.*"

"I don't know what happened last night. Your son says that he fell off a deer."

"Well, my son is not a liar."

"But he makes things up."

"Well, I don't think that's against the law." I could see my reflection in Sergeant Marino's silver badge.

"I just can't tell from what your son said if anything happened last night that I should know about."

"If my son said he fell off a deer, then that is what happened. He knows the difference between fantasy and reality."

At that point JB called out from the living room, "Darth Vader! Look!"

I turned to the policeman and smiled. "Well, he calls me that, you see, because I'm his father. You know, in the movie. '*Luke, I am your father.*' JB likes that part."

I entered the living room, and JB said, "Look," as he pointed to the television set. "Look at the cow flying." There was a cartoon about a cow jumping over the moon. "It's flying like the deer."

"Fantasy and reality, Mr. Kelly?" Sergeant Marino said, as he placed his hat on his head and walked toward the front door.

"Thank you for coming," Anna said, as she stood up from the couch. "I'll walk you out."

I sat down beside JB.

"Do you think the cow sat on a bumble bee?" JB asked.

"JB, how did you hurt your arm."

He looked at me and whispered, "Mr. Nicholas said I shouldn't tell too many people."

I froze.

"JB, what do you mean?"

"Mr. Nicholas said it would be bad for him if too many people found out about what happened."

"But you can tell me, JB."

He looked away from the television set and said, "I'll have to whisper."

As I leaned over, JB pulled my ear with his good hand, then he whispered, "I fell off the deer after it stopped flying around the tree."

Anna returned.

"So you had to call the police?" I asked.

"He's a very nice, responsible man."

"I was always nice, Anna."

"And responsible?"

"How was I to know that JB would sneak out of the house?"

"You can go now, Jim."

"But it's only Saturday. I have JB until Sunday night."

"The doctor said the best thing for JB is that he stays home and relaxes for a few days. I don't think driving down highways in the middle of the night and riding flying deer is much relaxation."

"Fine. You were always good at sarcasm. Fine. Keep the boy. Why don't you keep him all the time?"

"Because you are the boy's father."

JB looked up at me and said, "You're Darth Vader."

"I'll see you next Friday, JB."

He saluted. "Don't forget to feed the fish."

"Since when do you have fish?" Anna asked.

"I told you before. It's just something JB and I pretend. You know, Mr. Rogers' fish?"

"No. I don't."

"You have to learn to do a bit more pretending, Anna. You said so yourself. I am trying to change. You want me to see things more under the surface.

"It's hard to believe you, Jim. Once trust is broken it's hard to get it back."

"JB is teaching me to be more playful. To pretend more."

At the front door Anna said "Yes? Like pretending Mr. Nicholas didn't hurt my JB?"

"Goodbye, Anna. Have a good week."

"I'll find out about this Mr. Nicholas. We have to protect our children."

"Goodbye, Anna."

"Go feed your stupid fish!" And she slammed the door shut. I thought she could use more X-ray vision.

TWELVE

THE SECOND INVESTIGATION

If the police were going to conduct an investigation, and if Anna was going to conduct an investigation, then I was going to plan my own investigation. After all, I thought, I am a reporter, and I can get the facts just as well as, if not better than, anyone else.

It was no use interviewing JB any longer about the incident, for he just stuck to his story about the flying deer. And I didn't discover a great amount of information from the people in town when I asked what they knew about Mr. Nicholas. "He's an odd duck," a postman said.

"I'd like to know what really goes on in his basement," the mayor's husband said.

"He came here fifty-five years ago with nothing except a sleigh, some blankets and a beat-up old truck. I also know that he loves honey," Mrs. Murphy said. She was the oldest person living in town, and her memory was intact.

"He pays his taxes on time," the municipal clerk explained when I went to the hall of records, trying to learn more about Mr. Nicholas. "And he's been a good scavenger for the town all these years."

Most people I spoke with weren't very interested in Mr. Nicholas. They were more concerned about the snow, the bills, and Christmas shopping.

After I collected as much information about Mr. Nicholas as I could find, I wrote down all that I knew about him on separate pieces of yellow paper and taped each note to my kitchen wall. Every morning, before I took the bus to work, I'd look at all of my clues as I ate breakfast.

After thinking for a few days, and rereading my sketchy notes, I realized that I would have to interview Mr. Nicholas myself. I saw my chance when I looked out the bus window one Friday evening as Mr. Nicholas tried to post a sign outside the hardware store: CHRISTMAS BARN SALE SATURDAY: EVERYTHING MUST GO. The rumor was that the police were coming close to some conclusion about Mr. Nicholas' behavior, and that he was closing shop before anyone found out. As I said, JB knew all along, but who pays attention to a ten-year-old boy with Down syndrome who feeds Mr. Rogers' pretend fish?

I was on my way home from the city, having just completed an article on education. I was tired, distracted, and glad when the bus pulled down Main Street. As I stepped out from the bus, I saw Mr. Nicholas struggling with the sign, so I walked up to him and asked if he needed any help.

"If you could hold the sign in place while I nail it to the door," he said.

I placed my briefcase against the wall and held the sign. It was a heavy green sign with red letters.

"Up a little higher," Mr. Nicholas said. "Just a little more. Now turn it to the right a bit." He placed the nail at the top of the sign and then he gave the nail a few solid whacks with the hammer. "There. Done. Thank you very much."

I was about to pick up my briefcase and leave when Mr. Nicholas asked, "Is JB staying with you tonight?"

"Huh?" I asked, a bit puzzled that he knew about JB's weekend visits.

"Your son. He is your son, isn't he?"

"Yeah, he is," I said, as I once again began to leave.

"I never thanked you for helping me with the deer," he said, as he opened the door to his store.

"How's it doing?" I asked.

"Fine, fine. Would you like to see him?"

"Well, JB is coming soon. I should go home."

"It will only take a minute. I keep good track of time. Come on back through the store. I'll put a kettle on and you can have some coffee or tea. What do you drink?"

"I drink coffee," I said, as I once again leaned my briefcase against the wall and stepped into the dark store.

Mr. Nicholas's hardware store was closed for the night. There was just one center light hanging from the ceiling. It gave his store a mysterious amber glow, as if everything on the shelves and hanging on the wall was made of soft, yellow wax.

"Sure looks different in here without all the lights on," I said.

"Oh, your eyes adjust to the darkness soon enough. I've had lots of practice. Sometimes the moon helps."

"Yeah, the moon. I bet it just rolls down the aisle here and makes everything clear," I said, as I ran my hands over the paint cans, flashlights, and clothesline. Mr. Nicholas walked ahead of me, making his way through the store.

"Mr. Kelly, you should practice what you preach."

"Now what's that supposed to mean?" I asked, as I stopped in the middle of the aisle beside the power drills and screwdrivers.

"You should believe in the imagination a bit more." Mr. Nicholas turned and smiled.

"Yeah. That's what my wife says. What do you know about imagination?"

"Oh, a little, but you are much too hard on Mrs. Kelly."

"She's not so soft herself."

"Well, you shouldn't blame her if she's angry with you."

"How do you know that? Have you been talking to her, or that policeman? Have they been here already?"

"Oh, well, no, but I have a way of knowing things."

"Yeah. That's what my wife thinks. You know too much. Are you sure you're not some sort of ghost?"

"No, Mr. Kelly. Not a ghost."

"Well, let's just go see that deer," I said, as I came up to the open basement door. I stopped and looked down the narrow stairs.

"This way, Mr. Kelly," Mr. Nicholas said, as he closed the basement door and led me to the backyard.

"What do you have down there?"

"Oh, just a lot of inventory and a small workshop."

"Well I don't know about a workshop, but the whole town knows that you must have everything in that basement."

"Mr. Kelly, who do you think I am?"

"Well, that's what I came to find out. People are talking."

"Yes, they usually do, I'm afraid. Eventually they find out the truth, and things get bad for me."

"I don't mean to pry, Mr. Nicholas."

"Not at all. Just follow me."

He held the door open, and I stepped outside. I never saw the back of the hardware store. It was dark, and I tried to strain my eyes. I saw the oak tree JB spoke about, all right, but I couldn't see much else.

"Look hard, Mr. Kelly," Mr. Nicholas said. "Your eyes will adjust quickly. That is all Anna wants, for you to adjust your vision."

"I have twenty-twenty vision. I see just fine. And how do you know so much?"

"Just look hard, Jim. Look hard."

I squinted. I rubbed my eyes. I couldn't see much in the dark, but then slowly, I saw movement in the darkness beyond the tree, a large movement. "I see it. The deer we saved on the highway. Look at those antlers." I turned to Mr. Nicholas, but he just stared out beyond the darkness and nodded his head as if asking me to take another look. I did.

"What do you know about that," I said as I saw *two* deer with antlers under the oak tree. "Did you find another deer on the highway?"

Mr. Nicholas ran his hand through his beard and just smiled as he said, "Take another look, Mr. Kelly."

I looked into the yard again, and a bush turned into a third deer, and what I thought was a stump was a fourth deer sitting in the grass. A fifth deer suddenly nudged my leg and I jumped. They were all about the same size, small, but muscular and all sporting a full head of antlers. "What are you, some sort of highway deer doctor or something?" I asked, just as three more deer stepped up to where we stood. Mr. Nicholas reached into his pants pocket and gave them each a lump of sugar.

"Does the town know you have all these deer back here? I think there's a law about keeping wild animals."

"Oh, these are not wild, Mr. Kelly."

"Well, I don't know about that. I'm just wondering what you're doing with all these deer. And how come you're having a barn sale? Are you trying to skip out of town or something?"

"Things are beginning to catch up with me in a way. Why don't we go inside and have something to drink," Mr. Nicholas suggested.

I wondered if this was a good idea after all. "You know the police are watching you closely?"

"JB understands better than the police. I have no fear of them."

"Yeah, what it is with you and my son, and all those other kids? That's what I came here to find out in the first place. You know there are a lot of rumors about you these days."

"Let's go inside." Mr. Nicholas once again held open the door as I returned to the store.

"Just turn right. I live in the three rooms beyond the paint-shaking machine."

I walked into a little kitchen that smelled of gingerbread.

"Here. Sit at the table." Mr. Nicholas pulled out a chair as I sat down.

"What would you like? Milk? Hot chocolate? Coffee? Tea?"

"I could use something hot. Coffee. I can't stay long. JB will be coming soon. His mother's going to want to know about you."

"And I want to know more about her. She's not very happy, you know."

"Yeah. I think it started when she wanted to go to Paris and I wanted to go to a Yankees game."

Mr. Nicholas poured water into a kettle and placed it on the stove, and then he poured himself some milk in a glass. He walked over to a cupboard the size of one wall and opened two large doors. Inside the cupboard there must have been a thousand different plastic bags filled with cookies.

"You like cookies, I see," I said, trying to act unimpressed. I was startled, actually—all those cookies.

"Well, yes, in a way. People always give them to me. I can't eat them all at once, so I keep them here. They are partly to blame for my extra baggage." Then Mr. Nicholas patted his stomach and laughed a bit, and then he looked at me and laughed some more. I thought that was odd.

"You're a jolly person, Mr. Nicholas."

Mr. Nicholas reached into his shirt pocket and pulled out a pipe. "Is that the topic of one of your prepared questions for me?"

"So you could tell I came here for an investigation?"

"Mr. Kelly, you're a reporter," Mr. Nicholas said, as he poured my coffee into a mug, then lit his pipe.

"Yeah. Glad you reminded me. Let me just jot down a few things." I wrote on my pad *eight deer, likes cookies, drinks milk, has a workshop.* I looked up, then wrote, *smokes a pipe.*

"Where are you originally from?" I took a sip from my cup.

"Postcards and poetry, some people would think."

"Postcards, did you say?" I wrote on my pad, *postcards.* "What's poetry got to do with anything?"

"Mr. Kelly, do you ever watch *Mr. Rogers' Neighborhood*?"

"I did as a boy. I liked the land of Make-Believe and the trolley. JB watches all the time. Just the other night he fed Mr. Rogers' fish, like this." And then I demonstrated how I pinched a bit of food from the imaginary box and fed the fish.

"No, no, Mr. Kelly. Like this." And then Mr. Nicholas fed the imaginary fish in the exact same way as JB and Mr. Rogers.

"Hey, that's just like JB. Has he been here before? Have you been teaching him some things? Say, who are you anyway?"

"Santa Claus."

"Yeah. That's what JB said."

"You should listen to him more often."

"He's got Down syndrome."

"Jim, no . . . he's . . ."

"Yeah, I know. He's got me, and Anna."

"Do you like JB?" Mr. Nicholas asked.

"Say, who's doing the interview here?"

"Jim, do you like the boy?"

"Well, to be honest, I don't like him . . . I love him. And he loves me. He really is a Superboy and I *am* his father."

A clock, in the shape of a small wooden house in Mr. Nicholas's kitchen, struck seven. On each count, a small puff of smoke popped up from the clock's chimney.

"Say, how'd it do that?" I asked.

"It was difficult at first to synchronize the gears with the smoke, but then I built two small bellows inside that gave just the right action for the illusion."

I looked at Mr. Nicholas. "You like to make things?"

"Oh yes, I do. It's my hobby of sorts, I suppose."

I wrote on my pad *likes to build things*, and then I said, "I have to go home. JB will be there any minute."

As I stood up, Mr. Nicholas handed me a white bag with two large cookies in the shape of Santa Claus. "Take this home to JB," Mr. Nicholas suggested.

"Thanks. And thanks for the coffee and the tour. I'd check into the zoning about those deer."

"No need to worry, Mr. Kelly. I've got everything under control."

"Two little bellows?" I asked, as I took a closer look at the clock.

Mr. Nicholas just nodded his head up and down slightly.

"Well, what do you know about that. Who would have thought of such a thing? JB would like to see this someday. You mind if I come around and show him?"

"Why don't you stop by tomorrow? I have my Christmas sale."

"Yeah, the barn sale. That might be a good idea."

Mr. Nicholas walked me to the front of the store, and after we shook hands, he smiled and closed the door behind me. I leaned over, picked up my briefcase, and walked across the street to my apartment. It was snowing, and JB was waiting for me at the top of the stairs.

THIRTEEN
GOOD NIGHT, JB

Hi, Darth Vader."

"Hi, JB. Where's your mother?"

"She drove away."

He stuck out his tongue, trying to catch snow-flakes. "Can we order Chinese food?"

I unlocked my door, and JB and I walked into my apartment. "Chinese food coming up. What would you like?"

JB always asked for the same thing: sweet and sour chicken, an egg roll, and wonton soup.

As I looked up the number for the take-out food and dialed, I pulled out my white pad and scanned my list.

"Yes. Hello. I'd like to order two servings of sweet and sour chicken, two egg rolls, and two bowls of wonton soup." I grabbed my little yellow papers and began transferring my notes after I hung up the phone.

"It'll be ready in fifteen minutes, JB," I said, as I began taping the new information onto the kitchen wall: *hundreds of cookies, eight deer, milk, workshop in the basement.* Then I thought for a minute and wrote on another piece of yellow paper: *makes smoke come out of the clock.*

The phone rang.

"Hello." I held the receiver between my shoulder and ear, freeing my hands to complete my wall of evidence. "Hello, Anna."

"What did you find out?" she asked.

"About what?"

"Jim, you know perfectly well about what. That Mr. Nicholas."

I looked at the wall and gave Anna some of the facts I uncovered. "Well, he likes to make clocks. He does it as a hobby. You should see this clock he has in the kitchen. He built these small bellows right inside, and the smoke puffs out each time the clock strikes the hour."

"Jim, tell me something important."

I scanned my yellow bits of paper again. "Okay, this is all I've got. He drinks milk, he has a passion for cookies, he smokes a pipe, kids do seem to like him, he has a workshop, he's a scavenger, and he has eight deer."

"He has eight what?" Anna asked.

"These eight deer, he has eight deer in his backyard with these huge antlers."

JB curled his fingers and placed them on his head as he imitated what a deer with Down syndrome might look like. I did the same.

"Anna. The man is harmless. I spoke with him."

"What did he say?"

"He thinks that you're not a happy person."

There was a long pause at the other end of the line. Then Anna asked, "What are you having for dinner?"

"Chinese food."

"Sweet and sour chicken?" she asked.

This time it was my turn for a long pause. "Yeah."

"Remember how we liked ordering sweet and sour chicken every Saturday night?"

"And how cute JB looked with his lips all covered with the sauce?"

"Jim?"

"Yes?"

"He looked cute?"

"Yeah, and the way he smiled. Cute-like."

There was another pause.

"Anna?"

"I'll pick up JB Sunday night."

"Want to join us for dinner?"

Another long pause. "Well, maybe in the future. I'll pick up JB Sunday."

"Okay. I'll have him ready like always."

"Good night, Jim."

"Good night, Anna." I heard a click. I held onto the receiver for a few seconds longer, missing Anna's voice, and then I placed it back into the phone's cradle.

After JB and I ate our sweet and sour chicken, the egg roll, and soup, I tore open the small cellophane bag and gave JB a fortune cookie. I took one too. JB just bit into the cookie and suddenly had a small white tongue extending from his closed lips. He reached up and pulled the fortune out of his mouth and handed it to me.

"This is your fortune, JB: *What you see is what you get.*"

I looked at the boy and asked, "JB, what do you see?"

He grinned. "A stain on your shirt."

I looked down, and sure enough, there was a round stain in the center of my shirt. "Probably just some soup I spilled."

JB stood up, walked over to the couch, and sat down with a sigh. I opened a cookie and read my fortune: *Seek and you shall find*.

"Read *Ferdinand the Bull*," JB called from the couch. I walked over to the bookshelf and pulled down the pink and black book with the happy bull on the cover. I sat beside JB as he put his thumb in his mouth. "Once upon a time in Spain there was a little bull and his name was Ferdinand. . . ."

By the time I read the part about Ferdinand smelling the flowers, JB was asleep on the couch, his small head leaning against my shoulder like a limp watermelon. When he was born, I looked at his head. It was an odd shape, a small globe, a shape of a distorted egg, surely a distortion of some sort, though I could not identify it right away. When I looked at JB through the nursery window, I saw the other babies crying, kicking, and throwing their little hands up in the air. JB just lay back limp in the small bassinet, like Ferdinand, just rolling back, smelling the flowers.

I picked him up in my arms, this solid boy in blue jeans and a sweatshirt. His hair was out of place; a bit of drool rolled down the side of his mouth. I placed him in bed, and he rolled to his side. I pulled the blanket up to his shoulders and kissed his head and said quietly, "I love you, JB." As I stepped out of the room, I heard a small whisper, "Good night, Darth Vader."

Because I was concerned about JB getting up in the middle of the night and wandering out of the apartment again, I locked the back door, and then I tied a small brass bell to the door handle. If JB tried to leave, the bell would wake me up.

FOURTEEN

TO THE BARN

The next morning, when I looked at the clock on my nightstand and saw that it was 9:17, I panicked. "JB?" I called out, as I ran to his room. His bed was empty. "JB?" I called out again, as I ran down the hall. "JB?" I didn't hear the bell ring in the night. I turned the corner, and there, sitting at the kitchen table, was JB. "I made breakfast."

The table was set for two. There was a cookie on my plate, the cookie from Mr. Nicholas, and a full glass of milk sitting beside a folded napkin. JB's Santa Claus cookie was half eaten, and he had already finished his glass of milk. "I ate some of my cookie." JB smiled.

I looked at him across the table and he just grinned.

I picked up the cookie and observed JB's split lips, his crooked eyes, his silly smile, then I looked up at all my yellow notes stuck to the kitchen wall. "Eight deer. Likes to smoke a pipe. Likes cookies. Has a workshop." Then I brought the cookie to my lips, and bit off Santa's legs. JB laughed.

"We're going to Mr. Nicholas's barn sale."

"Will he have chocolate?" JB asked.

"You like Mr. Nicholas, don't you?"

"He's my friend," JB answered.

"Yeah. I like him too."

After I showered, JB dressed himself. I had to help him with his shirt. He slipped it on his head backwards. When I pulled on my socks, he imitated me and pulled on his socks. When I combed my hair, he pretended that he combed his hair. I ran my comb in his hair, and then I said, "We have to feed the fish."

JB took my hand and led me into the living room. We sat on the couch, and JB pinched a bit of imaginary food and slowly waved the small, imaginary flakes down into the calm, still water of the imaginary fish tank.

By the time JB and I walked across the street, there was already a great crowd of people milling about under a large banner, CHRISTMAS BARN SALE. Mr. Nicholas priced everything seventy to eighty percent off the regular prices.

"Looks like Mr. Nicholas is ready to skip town," Charlie said, with a pleased grin. But his grin quickly turned sour when he saw a brand-new, blue Weil-McLain furnace with a $58.00 price tag.

People bought bags of grass seed, snow shovels, wheelbarrows. JB and I wandered inside the barn. Rakes hung from the rafters. Balls of rope and spools of wire were priced at a nickel apiece. Everything was being sold. As I looked through a box filled with pliers and screwdrivers, JB called out from the back of the barn. "Let's buy this!" He was sitting in an antique sleigh made of polished wood and thin, silver runners. The seat was made of velvet. Mr. Nicholas stepped up from behind me as I ran my hand along the side of the sleigh.

"That's not for sale," Mr. Nicholas said with a smile.

"It's beautiful," I said. "What type of wood is it made from?"

"Oak from California, teak from India. Here is a bit of a palm tree, and here a Japanese maple. There is the wood of the African banyan tree and the South American banana tree, Russian maples, apple wood from Vermont."

JB looked down at me from the seat of the sleigh, grinning. Mr. Nicholas reached up to JB with a closed hand. JB extended his open, fat little hand, and Mr. Nicholas gave JB a bit of chocolate wrapped in gold foil. JB jumped down from the sleigh. I bought a set of screwdrivers. Just before we left, I turned to Mr. Nicholas and asked, "Russian maple?"

Mr. Nicholas nodded.

"Banyan tree from Africa?"

Mr. Nicholas smiled. I looked at his eyes, his beard, the suspenders, and then he just laughed and laughed. In two hours the barn was empty, except for the single antique sleigh.

JB unwrapped his bit of chocolate. It was in the shape of a fish. It began to snow.

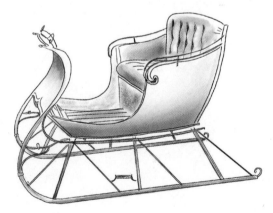

FIFTEEN
I LOVE YOU

Jim, why don't you go first? What have you been thinking this past week?"

I looked at Dr. Matthews, my arms unfolded, my hands resting on my lap. "Upcoming Christmas and a few deadlines at work. Nothing special."

"I mean about your and Anna's separation."

I turned to look at Anna. "She likes sweet and sour chicken."

"Anna, is there anything you'd like to say?"

Instead of looking at the counselor, Anna looked at me. "Jim said that he thinks JB is cute."

"He is cute. You should have seen him when I picked him up in his blue jeans and sweatshirt."

"Is that all?" Dr. Matthews asked.

I folded my arms. "I was reading aloud *Ferdinand the Bull*, that's all."

"Jim, there's more," Dr. Matthews said.

"Jim," Anna added, "you said to me on the phone that JB was cute."

"Well, he was," I said. "I picked him up in my arms. His hair was combed. His drool at the corner of his mouth, I can't explain it. I smiled." I unfolded my arms as my right hand rested on the couch.

"Jim?" Anna said as she placed her left hand on top of mine.

I looked into Anna's eyes. "I placed JB on his bed." Anna's eyes watered. "He rolled to his side. I pulled his Star Wars blanket up to his shoulders and kissed him on the head and whispered, 'I love you.'"

I sat on the couch. Dr. Matthews looked at me, and then I turned and leaned into Anna, and then I just cried and whispered, "We can be a family."

SIXTEEN

THE VISIT

Anna and I made a deal for Christmas. I would have JB for Christmas Eve, and she would have him Christmas Day. I looked out the window, waiting for JB that early night of December 24th. It was snowing. The hardware store was closed for two weeks. The large banner still hung above the barn. Mr. Nicholas always took his vacation during the last two weeks of December.

The sidewalk was illuminated with a line of streetlamps decorated with Christmas wreaths. Everything was closed. I saw, in the distance, bright headlights cutting through the falling snow. The car pulled up to my building, and JB tumbled out from the passenger side with his Star Wars lunch box. He looked up and opened his mouth, trying to catch snowflakes on his tongue, and then he began climbing the stairs to my apartment. When I opened the door, he tried to talk with his tongue extended out from his mouth. "Tee? Tee?"

"What, JB?" I asked.

He pointed to his tongue and repeated "Tee?"

"Oh, yeah. I *see*. The snowflakes."

JB pulled his tongue back into his mouth and gulped, pretending he had just swallowed a mouthful of Christmas snow. "Let's have Chinese food," he said.

As JB and I ate our sweet and sour chicken, we watched Mr. Rogers pet a kitten, sit on the swing, and talk with a poet, and then he sang. JB could never snap his fingers, so when Mr. Rogers sang, "I think I'll make a snappy new day," JB clapped twice.

After the visit with Mr. Rogers, JB hung up his stocking on the doorknob of the kitchen door, and then he opened the refrigerator and pulled out the jug of milk. JB pushed a chair to the cupboard, climbed the chair, and reached for a glass on the shelf. He placed the glass on the floor by the back door and filled it with milk. He returned to the chair, and reached up for a small plate, then he pulled out a pack of Oreo cookies and placed the plate on the floor next to the glass of milk. Then JB placed three cookies on the empty plate. He returned to me and reached up his arms. I bent down, picked him up, and carried him to his bed.

When JB was settled under the blanket, he said, "Good night, Darth Vader."

"Good night, my Luke Skywalker," I said, as I leaned over and kissed his round cheek.

"I rode Comet around the tree," JB said.

I thought about the little bellows and the smoke huffing and puffing out of the chimney of the little kitchen clock. I thought about my wall notes. JB was asleep.

After I washed dishes and straightened up the living room, I pulled out JB's presents from the closet and arranged them under the small tree I had bought at the gas station. Then I went to bed.

In the middle of the night I was roused a bit, and I heard a bell ringing in the distance. At first, I thought it was just the sound of my dream, but then there was a clatter, and I recognized the sound of the doorknob bell. *JB! He's run away again*, I thought with a panic.

"JB!" I called out, as I ran from my bed and into his room. "JB!" There he was, under his blanket, sleeping with his panda bear.

I stepped into the living room, and was startled to find Mr. Nicholas standing by the door. "Sorry about the noise. You know that you have a bell tied to the door handle," he said, with an annoyed whisper.

"It's my JB alarm. Ever since he ran out that night I worried about him doing it again."

I looked at the little man as he brushed the snow and soot from the shoulders of his little red coat. "You're not just a hardware salesman, are you?" I asked.

"Jim, there's lots you don't know, but if you do your homework, pay attention, and add up the facts, you will figure things out," he said, as he looked at my wall of yellow notes.

"That's what my third-grade teacher always said."

"She was a very wise woman, and she made the most delicious chocolate chip cookies."

"You knew her, I suppose?"

"Who?" Mr. Nicholas asked, as he slung a burlap sack onto the floor of the kitchen.

"Mrs. Houston, my third-grade teacher?"

"Oh, of course. I know everyone."

"I'm not sure what I know anymore. Maybe I'm having a dream, and you're just undigested sweet and sour chicken."

"No, I'm real," Mr. Nicholas said, as he pulled out from his sack a large box wrapped in red paper and tied in a green bow.

"I'm not sure I like this, you coming in here in the middle of the night. You know the police are watching you very closely."

"Jim, do you remember seeing JB for the first time?"

"Sure I do."

"Do you remember what you thought?" Mr. Nicholas asked, as he carried the box and placed it under the tree.

"I thought he was so different, not what I was expecting. I was deeply disappointed."

"When was the first time you didn't feel that?"

"I'll tell you when: when you and I were carrying the deer up from the ditch and JB was standing there in his sombrero. That was the first time I ever said to myself, 'What a cute kid.'"

"People do it all the time," Mr. Nicholas said, as he pulled out a small box and placed it under the tree. "They look at a person and make snap judgments. I'm sorry I never got to know Anna better."

"What does she have to do with all this?"

"You don't know, Jim?"

"Know? Know what?"

"She still loves you."

"Yeah, and you're Santa Claus, I suppose," I said without thinking, and then I looked at Mr. Nicholas as he adjusted his white gloves.

"I must be going," he said.

I looked into his eyes. "This would make a great story for the newspaper, but my editor would fire me for being a lunatic."

"You are a lunatic, Jim. Most of us are, except people like JB. Some people look at him and think he is useless. But JB is a messenger. The world tries to bend him to its ways, but the way of the child is not the way of the world, and only until we learn the ways of the child will we inherit the earth."

Mr. Nicholas adjusted his red hat, picked up his sack, and stepped into the kitchen. As he looked at my yellow notes, he said, "Do not forget to feed the fish, Jim."

He leaned over and picked up the three cookies. "Oreos! One of my favorites." Then he drank the milk JB had poured for him, laughed, shook my hand, and walked down the narrow stairs to the street. I looked out the window and watched as Mr. Nicholas climbed into his sleigh. He shook the reins and waved as eight deer began pulling him down the street. I waved back as I watched Mr. Nicholas disappear into the driving snow, but I could still hear, for a few moments, the ringing of the sleigh bells, ringing, ringing, ringing. . . .

SEVENTEEN

CHRISTMAS DAY

I reached over and shut off my alarm clock. It was Christmas morning. JB ran into my room, bounced on my bed, and said, "Let's open the presents." He grabbed my hand and dragged me into the living room. He unwrapped the things I bought for him first: a *Star Wars* light saber, a Disney plush toy: Bambi, a Mr. Rogers' DVD of a visit to a construction site, and a baseball cap. His stocking was filled with chocolate reindeer wrapped in gold foil.

When there were two gifts left under the tree, both from Mr. Nicholas, JB said, "Open yours first."

I picked up the small box, pulled the red bow, opened the lid, reached in, and pulled out the clock that hung in Mr. Nicholas's kitchen.

"It's a little house," JB said.

I smiled. "If you look inside, you can see two little bellows," I whispered, forgetting that JB would have no idea what bellows were, but he looked inside just the same. Then he shouted, "Hey! There I am!" I was startled. I leaned over, cheek to cheek with JB as we both peered into the little house. There was, indeed, a small boy sitting on a couch holding a book in his hand, and a man and a woman sitting on either side of the boy. I opened a drawer and pulled out a magnifying glass and looked again into the house. The little book in the boy's hand was *Ferdinand the Bull*. On the bottom of the gift box I found an envelope, and inside the envelope was a card. A portrait of Henry David Thoreau was on the cover, and inside the card were these words that I read aloud: *The keeping of bees is like the direction of sunbeams. Merry Christmas, Jim. Mr. Nicholas.*

JB looked at me and said, "I hope Ferdinand doesn't sit on those bees." Then he said, "My turn," as he leaned over and dragged the large box beside him. He reached up, pulled the green ribbon, and tore away the wrapping paper. There, sitting before us, was a fish tank filled with water and three small goldfish swimming about happily. JB also found a box of fish food.

He opened the box, pinched a bit between his fingers and waved his hand over the tank back and forth, just like Mr. Rogers.

"Now you, Daddy," JB said. It was the first time in a long time that JB had called me Daddy.

I, too, waved my hand back and forth over the fish tank.

A car door slammed shut. JB looked out the window. "It's Mom."

I stood up from the floor and saw Anna step around the car and walk purposefully toward the building.

"Maybe we better not tell Mom where you got the fish, JB."

JB ran to the back door as we both heard Anna climbing the stairs. JB opened the door and embraced his mother when she reached the top. "Mr. Nicholas brought me fish for Christmas!"

Anna looked up at me.

"I can explain. He just wanted to do something nice for JB. There's no harm in that, is there?"

Anna stood up and said, "No, there's no harm in that," and then she embraced me, kissed me, and started to cry.

"Anna?"

She looked at me.

"Anna, what's wrong?"

"Nothing. Absolutely nothing. Thank you for my Christmas gift."

I didn't get anything for Anna. "Yeah, sure, ah, I'm glad you liked it."

"When I opened the mail . . . Where did you get such a wonderful card?" She asked, as she pulled out the envelope from her coat pocket.

I took it from her hand and pulled out the card. It was made of gold foil with a painting of Mr. Nicholas's blue hardware store embossed in the center. I opened the card and found three round-trip tickets to France with a note, in *my* handwriting, "Let's go to Paris as I promised."

"The three of us?" Anna asked.

"Yes, the three of us," I said.

Anna embraced me and said, "When we get back, let's you and I take JB out for sweet and sour chicken." And then Anna handed me shredded pieces of paper from her other pocket. It was the separation documents.

I leaned over and kissed her tenderly. "I see you, Anna, and I love you."

"Come feed my fish!" JB called out, as he ran into the living room. "They're hungry."

JB grabbed my right hand, and he grabbed Anna's left hand as he pulled us together toward the fish tank, where three goldfish happily swam in and out of a small plaster castle.

"Merry Christmas, Jim," Anna said, as she watched the fish swim to the top of the water.

"Merry Christmas, Anna," I said, as I watched Anna's eyes tear up.

"Merry Christmas, Darth Vader," JB said, as he waved his magical hand and sprinkled fish food over the calm surface of the water.

"Merry Christmas, JB," I said. "Merry Christmas, my Superboy."

EIGHTEEN
PARIS

There is a boy feeding the fish in the Tuileries Garden in Paris. His mother and father are standing beside him.

"Here," JB says to his mother. "Now you feed them."

Anna reaches into the bag of breadcrumbs and tosses the food into the water.

"No," JB says. "You gotta do it like this, like Mr. Rogers," and he pinches some breadcrumbs between his fingers and gently waves his hand back and forth across the water.

Then I begin feeding the fish until Anna pulls my sleeve. "Jim?"

I turn around and see a French policeman strolling up behind us. He is short, has a white beard, and is bit overweight. He looks familiar.

Anna whispers, "Maybe we're not allowed to do this."

"Ah, excusez-moi," I say. "We didn't know."

"No, no, monsieur. It is quite all right. Never forget to feed the fish. The children, they always remember how. Bonjour." JB salutes, as the policeman tips his hat, winks, and continues on his way.

ACKNOWLEDGMENTS

Mr. Nicholas is a universal story of faith, goodness and hope, and such stories are never written in isolation. The French Nobel Prize-winning author André Gide wrote that "art is a collaboration between God and the artist, and the less the artist does, the better."

All I did was write a little story. Jon Sweeney of Paraclete Press and his team took a bit of rough marble and chiseled a physically beautiful book. My daughter, Karen, a graduate of Rutgers University with a major in English, and a PhD in being a daughter, greatly helped with the editing process, refining Mr. Nicholas's voice and laughter.

I am grateful to my wife, Roe, for her support and love and for her turning our small sun porch into my little writing space off the living room.

And I am grateful that someday our grandson, Finnian, will read this book and remember how much his grandfather loved him.

I could not have written this book had it not been for a forty-year friendship with Robbie Jones, a man of humor, generosity and wisdom, the unofficial mayor of our little town, Santa on the fire truck each December, and the proprietor of our local hardware store that doesn't exist any longer except in the memory and hearts of everyone in town.

And I am in debt to the voice of Jimmy Stewart in the film *It's A Wonderful Life,* and to Joanne and Fred Rogers for their consistent faith in children, innocence, and purity of heart.

I acknowledge a community that surrounds a book: writers, editors, readers, family, and friends.

Mark Twain wrote "The *almost right* word and the *right* word is really a large matter. 'Tis the difference between the lightning bugs and the lightning."

God is the lightning and we, citizens of goodness, just light small candles along the way to help make the darkness less fearsome.

Oh, and don't forget to feed the fish.

ABOUT PARACLETE PRESS

PARACLETE PRESS is the publishing arm of the Cape Cod monastic community, the Community of Jesus. Presenting a full expression of Christian belief and practice, we reflect the ecumenical charism of the Community and its dedication to sacred music, the fine arts, and the written word.

Learn more about us at our website
www.paracletepress.com
or phone us toll-free at 1.800.451.5006

SCAN
TO
READ
MORE

ANOTHER CHRISTMAS NOVEL YOU MAY ENJOY...

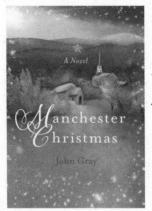

Manchester Christmas
A Novel
John Gray

ISBN 978-1-64060-640-1
Hardcover | $22

Young writer Chase Harrington is drawn to a small New England town in search of meaning for her life. Soon, she encounters kindness, romance, and a mystery centered on an old, abandoned church and the death of a special girl. Full of love, hope, and forgiveness, *Manchester Christmas* illustrates how God often uses the most unlikely among us to spread grace and healing in a wounded world.

"Sweet, romantic, and suspenseful,
Manchester Christmas is an unexpected gift."
—**Richard Paul Evans**, #1 *New York Times* Bestselling
Author of *The Christmas Box*

Available at bookstores
Paraclete Press | 1-800-451-5006
www.paracletepress.com